Sally B
...& ME!

F.J. Beerling

Illustrated by Gareth Bowler

Fairyfaye Publications
ISBN: 9781999752071

ISBN: 9781999752071

Published by Fairyfaye Publications
For events and all enquiries email fairyfayepublications@gmail.com

Edited by Denise Smith www.dspublishingservices.co.uk

Very special thanks to
Elly Sallingboe without whom this book would not have been possible.

Poetic licence has been applied on occasion!

Book design by Gareth Bowler

Printed in Great Britain

Dedicated to the memory of my beloved sister
Elisabeth Sallingboe Dinesen
whose guidance and love is missed beyond words
- and to all who cares for Sally B.

-Elly Sallingboe-

B-17 Flying Fortress – Sally B

For over 40 years, Europe's last remaining airworthy B-17 Flying Fortress,
Sally B, has graced British skies as a flying memorial to the
79,000 US and Allied airmen who lost their lives
fighting for our freedom in Europe during World War Two.
Keeping a huge 4 engined B-17 flying for forty plus years is an outstanding
achievement for the aircraft's operator and guardian, Elly Sallingboe of
B-17 Preservation, who with the help of her crew and team of volunteers
have kept Sally B flying without any official help since 1982.
Enthusiasm, dedication and sheer determination has made the 'impossible' possible.
Sally B is based at the Imperial War Museum, Duxford from where she is on
static display when not flying. She is backed by a registered charity,
'The B-17 Charitable Trust' and aided solely by public donations
and the support of the 6,500 members of the Sally B Supporters club.
This is the only B-17 in the world run totally on public donations and true passion.
For more information on the aircraft and how you can help, contact Elly at:

www.sallyb.org.uk

They called it the 'Flying Fortress',
And built it for World War II,
Then loaded it up with guns and bombs,
And into the air it flew.

This was the famous B17,
And its mission during that war
Was to save Europe from enemy invasion,
Which was done with airplanes galore.

They flew into the enemy
And shot them from the sky;
Propelled by four big engines,
Dropping bombs, then flying high.

And on a single tank of fuel,
They flew 2,000 miles.
With speeds of 200 miles an hour,
They crossed the British Isles!

But not every Flying Fortress
To come off the production line
Was loaded up with guns and bombs,
And made it to war on time.

The year was1945
When newly built Sally B was made too late to serve in the war;
Could this be the end of her story?

Destined for the scrapheap?
Or would she be taken apart?
124485
108
Bonjour...
No – Sally B was taken to France,
Where her life in flight would start.

Happily flying for many years,
And when that job was done,
A businessman brought her and she came to England,
Where another adventure had begun...

The businessman, Ted, named her Sally B;
that's how she got her name.
And even though he almost sold her, their lives were about to change...

...When Elly met her, she fell in love, and desperately wanted to fly.
So they both worked hard spending many hours in airplanes, up in the sky.

...And Sally B was named after Elly!

So restored to wartime glory,
And with an important job to do,
Sally B would tell the history
Of B17s and their crew:

Of how they flew for many miles,
And how they paid the cost,
When they stopped the enemy invading;
And many pilots' lives were lost.

And back in 1975
Into the air she went.
Sally B flew at air shows
And over Biggin Hill Airport in Kent.

Sally B

G-ELLY

Elly and Ted had many dreams
For Sally B and her crew.
But then one day, Ted went away,
And into the clouds he flew.

Elly's world was shattered;
How would she cope all alone?
But when she looked, and saw Sally B,
She realised she wasn't alone.

Elly kept Sally B up in the air,
And the crowds would clap and cheer.

She even flew, along with the crew,
On D-Day in the same year!

She also flew over Poland,
And went to Holland as well,

And in the UK, was a flying memorial
To the American airmen who fell.

But back in 1998,
When things were looking bad,
Stranded, and many miles from home,
Sally B was ever so sad.

Would she ever fly again?
Did anybody care?
Of course they did, especially Elly,
Because Elly was always there...

She knocked on doors and asked around,
And engineering help was found.
She needed warmth and a place to stay;
Elly's hotel bed wasn't too far away.

She booked flights and tickets, and gathered together a crew,
And they fixed Sally B until she was as good as new.

And for many years,
And many miles,
Through heartache,
Tears, and lots of smiles,
And against all odds,
And out of love,
Elly kept Sally B flying above.

She did it by raising thousands of pounds, and this has kept them going.
Delighting so many as she flew past and Sally B is still showing!

So many supporters have loved her, and for more than forty years
It was Elly and a team that kept her flying,
Through the good times, and the tears...

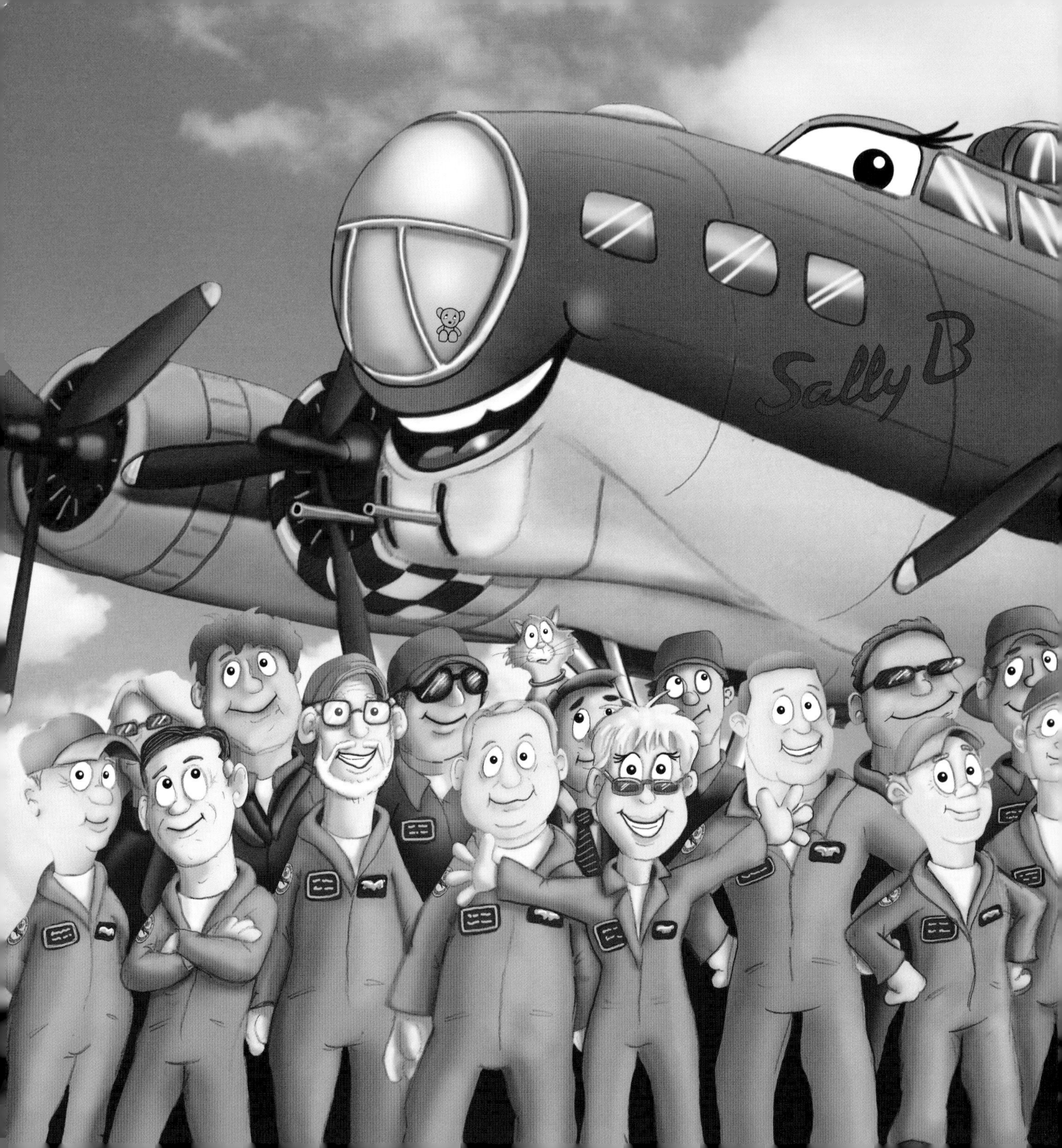
Sally B

... From the engineers that fixed her,
To the support team on the ground,
And all her members who loved her;
Everyone rallied around!

And they have kept her flying,
She still flies high above,
So THANK YOU to the Sally B family
For giving their time and so much love!

Starring Sally B as...

Memphis Belle

From 'Flying Fortress' to 'film star';
Sally B starred in 'Memphis Belle'.
She even starred in 'We'll Meet Again'
And other big movies as well.

But it costs a fortune to fly her;
She needs fuel as well as love...

Sally B
x
Memphis Belle

...So please donate, even in a small way,
To keep her flying above.